For my goddaughter, Harmoni.
Stay a princess as long as you can.

Little, Brown and Company
Hachette Book Group
1290 Avenue of the Americas, New York, NY 10104
Visit us at LBYR.com

Originally published in 2014 by CreateSpace Independent Publishing Platform in the United States of America
First Little, Brown Edition: October 2017

Little, Brown and Company is a division of Hachette Book Group, Inc.
The Little, Brown name and logo are trademarks of Hachette Book Group, Inc.

The publisher is not responsible for websites (or their content) that are not owned by the publisher.

ISBNs: 978-0-316-56261-4 (hardcover), 978-0-316-44099-8 (ebook), 978-0-316-56256-0 (ebook), 978-0-316-44120-9 (ebook)

Printed in China

1010

10 9 8 7 6

The illustrations for this book were created using watercolor and ink and were digitally finished.
This book was edited by Kheryn Callender and designed by Jamie W. Yee with art direction by Saho Fujii.
The production was supervised by Erika Schwartz, and the production editor was Marisa Finkelstein.
The text was set in Barthowheel, and the display type was hand-lettered.

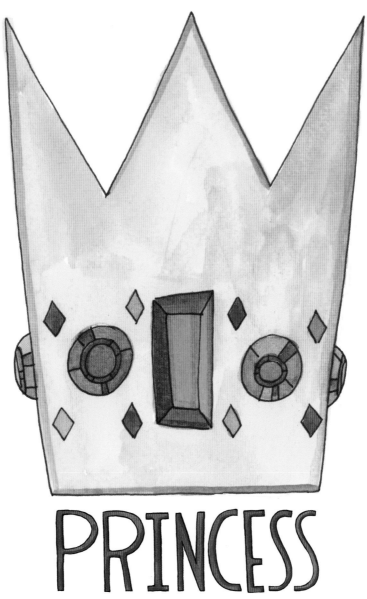

PRINCESS HAIR

BY SHAREE MILLER

LITTLE, BROWN AND COMPANY
NEW YORK BOSTON

All princesses wear crowns,

but underneath their crowns, not
all princesses have the same hair.

Some princesses wear **PUFFS** and play pretend.

Others wear **TWIST OUTS** and twirl around.

Princesses with **DREADLOCKS** love

to draw
and draw
and draw.

Princesses with KINKS love to think!

And princesses with

FROHAWKS rock!

Princesses with **HEAD WRAPS** take long naps.

Princesses with CURLS wear pearls.

And princesses with
TEENY-WEENY AFROS
wear teeny-weeny bows.

Princesses with BANTU KNOTS
bake a LOT!

Princesses with **AFROS** do-si-do.

Princesses with BRAIDS throw parades!

Princesses with BUNS
love to run.

Princesses with
BLOWOUTS

bounce and bounce and bounce.

Princesses with **TWISTS** wrap gifts.

And NAPPY Princesses are HAPPY Princesses.

Not every Princess has the same hair.

But every Princess **LOVES** her Princess hair!